MW01045396

THE
PACK

SUSANNAH BRIN

Artesian Press

P.O. Box 355, Buena Park, CA 90621

Take Ten Books
Horror

From the Eye of the Cat	1-58659-071-5
Cassette	1-58659-076-6
The Indian Hills Horror	1-58659-072-3
Cassette	1-58659-077-4
The Oak Tree Horror	1-58659-073-1
Cassette	1-58659-078-2
The Pack	**1-58659-074-X**
Cassette	**1-58659-079-0**
Return to Gallows Hill	1-58659-075-8
Cassette	1-58659-080-4

Other Take Ten Themes:

Mystery
Sports
Adventure
Chillers
Thrillers
Disaster
Fantasy
Romance

Project Editor: Dwayne Epstein
Illustrations: Fujiko
Graphic Design: Tony Amaro
©2001 Artesian Press

www.artesianpress.com

 ISBN 1-58659-074-X

Contents

Chapter 1 5

Chapter 2 9

Chapter 3 13

Chapter 4 19

Chapter 5 25

Chapter 6 31

Chapter 7 35

Chapter 8 39

Chapter 9 46

Chapter 10 53

Chapter 1

Candle Selky frowned as she stared at the old ranch house.

"It's not so bad," Lucinda said. She put her arm around her daughter Candle's shoulder.

"Nothing a bulldozer can't fix," Bane said as he joined them.

"Bane, you're awful," Lucinda laughed. She went into the house.

"I wish for once we could buy a new house with fresh paint and a front lawn," Candle sighed.

"Forget it, Candle. We are never going to be like other people," Bane said.

Candle looked at her brother, Bane. He was seventeen, a year older than she, and he was so sure of himself. Once they were as close as most brothers and sisters. Now, it seemed as though they were always arguing.

In her room, Candle hung up her clothes, put her few books on a shelf, and made her bed. Carefully, she picked two framed photos out of a box. One photo was of her father. The other one was of a silvery black wolf. Candle walked to the open window.

The hot sun was beginning to go down behind the mountains, making long, purple shadows on the desert floor.

Car horns honked in the yard. *The family has arrived*, thought Candle. She saw her cousins, aunts, and uncles getting out of vans and cars. Sonny Wendig, the loner who had forced his way into their family and become leader, was there, too.

Candle thought about her father. He was the leader of the family until he was shot by a farmer's bullet that crippled him. Then he died after a fight with Sonny.

6

"Mother wants us to come downstairs and say 'hello' to Sonny and the others," Bane said from the doorway.

"I have nothing to say to that man," Candle said angrily. Her black eyes were flashing with anger. She shook her head, making her long silvery blonde hair fly around her shoulders.

Bane ran his fingers through his own silvery blond hair. "At least we agree on something. We will just have to ignore him until . . ."

"Until what?" Candle asked. Her stomach felt tight. "Can't we just live like other people?"

Bane said with disgust, "You can't change who you are, Candle."

Candle knew there was no use in arguing with Bane. They wanted different things.

The huge living room was noisy with relatives. Candle stayed at the edge of the room, waiting to escape back to her own room.

"Listen, everyone," Sonny shouted. " I just want to say, I hope we will all be happy here. We have four hundred acres. A lot of room to roam." He flashed a brilliant smile of perfect white teeth. "We'll start building more homes and a community hall soon. Until then, we'll use the barn for meetings."

Candle watched her mother walk Sonny Wendig to the door. "Why does she even talk to him?" she said to herself.

Bane stared at Sonny's back. "If he knows what's good for him, he'll hang around someplace else."

Candle frowned as she climbed the stairs to her room. She was sick of her family, sick of her life as a member of the pack. She wanted to be normal and just live a normal human life.

Chapter 2

"Did you hear the coyotes howling last night?" Tomas Alvarez asked. He looked at his friend, David Payne.

David stopped wiping the golf cart. He turned and said, "Nope, I was so tired last night, I slept like the dead."

Tomas grinned. "You're soft, man."

"Oh, yeah? Well, I wasn't the one riding in an air-conditioned car all day, picking up supplies for the pro shop. I was out on the golf course digging up sprinkler lines," said David.

"I forgot," Tomas said, grinning.

David jumped into the golf cart and drove it down the hill to where the cleaned carts waited in line to be rented.

Tomas picked up the hose and washed the tires of another cart.

"So what were you saying about the

coyotes?" David asked as he walked back up the hill.

"Their howling is louder, like the packs have grown bigger or something. It's strange, man," Tomas said. He looked at the desert surrounding the beautiful green golf course.

"You aren't scared of a pack of coyotes, are you?" David asked.

Tomas frowned. "No. I just have this feeling something weird is going on in the desert at night."

"What's weird is that huge family moving into the old Double R Ranch," David said. "How often do you hear of an extended family all living in one place? My relatives would kill each other if they all lived together."

Tomas laughed. "In my family, we think the more the merrier."

"You boys can go after you sweep up the range balls," Bill Biggs said stepping out of the pro shop. "And bring in all the wire buckets."

"No problem, Mr. Biggs," Tomas smiled.

David picked up a bucket of soapy water and emptied it in the flowerbed. He looked at the pro shop, then at Tomas. "Man, you are always trying to look good in front of the boss."

Tomas's dark eyes widened playfully. "Just trying to be polite, that's all. Besides, I need this job."

"Yeah, me, too. I just wish it paid more," David complained. They walked toward the driving range where golfers practiced hitting buckets of balls.

"Not too many jobs around here for sixteen-year-olds like us, you know. At least we can play golf for free and swim in the pool after hours," said Tomas cheerfully.

"My pickup truck needs work. The tires are so bald, I'm almost driving on the rims," David said.

At the driving range, David jumped on the tractor. It had a rake that

11

gathered the golf balls. Tomas stacked the wire baskets and then helped David unload the range balls into a large container. A howl echoed across the darkening desert.

"That sounds more like a wolf than a coyote," David said. He dumped the last of the balls into the container.

"How can you tell the difference?" Tomas asked. He stared at the canyons that went through the mountain.

"I'm not sure it's a wolf, but coyotes tend to yip a couple times then howl," David explained.

"How do you know all this stuff, man?" Tomas asked.

David shrugged. "My dad."

"Oh, yeah, I forgot he's a park ranger. Ask him if there are wolves around here," Tomas said.

Suddenly, the howling turned into a terrible scream. Somewhere in the desert, one animal was killing another.

Chapter 3

The next night, Candle went with Bane and their cousin Ralphie into Desert Springs. As they drove down the main street, she sighed—another small town in the middle of nowhere.

Bane and Ralphie saw two girls entering the cafe. "Want a burger?" Bane asked. He drove the van into the parking lot.

"I could think of something tastier than a burger," Ralphie growled playfully.

"Don't even think like that," Candle said. Thoughts lead to actions, and actions in her family left people dead.

Bane grinned. "He's joking. We know better than to start something so close to home."

Candle looked at Bane, wondering if he knew what really happened at their last home. Had he, or one of the cousins, killed those teenagers camping in the woods? Is that what angered the people of the town and sent them on a wolf- killing spree?

The story was that the farmers were upset over the death of some sheep. No people had been killed, but Candle wasn't sure she believed it. Her father was shot in the leg, and later, Sonny Wendig killed him.

Rushing into the cafe, Candle bumped into a boy. Soda pop splashed on her arm and clothes.

"Gosh, I'm sorry," said David Payne.

"My fault," Candle said, feeling her face get hot.

David grabbed some napkins. "Here, use these," he said.

Candle wiped off her arm, her tank top, and shorts.

David stared at Candle. She was the most beautiful girl he'd ever seen. "Can

14

Candle bumped into David, splashing soda all over her arm and clothes.

I buy you a soda or something to make up for ruining your clothes?" David asked nervously.

Candle smiled, "I'm okay, really."

"Please," David said.

Candle heard Bane and Ralphie laughing behind her, and she was angry. She knew they were talking about her. She smiled sweetly at David. "I'll have an orange freeze."

As they waited for the freeze, they introduced themselves. David told her he lived in town. She explained they'd just moved into the Double R Ranch.

"How do you like it here so far?" he asked.

"The desert is quite pretty. I was surprised to see all the wildflowers and small animals," Candle answered.

Bane listened in and laughed. "My sister really likes small animals," he said, walking over to them.

Candle took a deep breath to control her anger. "We'll be outside," Bane said. He looked at David's smaller size, decided he would be no trouble, and he and Ralphie walked out.

"Sorry. My brother and cousin are jerks," Candle said.

"Likes to tease you, I bet," David said as he handed her the orange freeze.

"Yeah. Thanks," Candle said, taking the cold drink. "I've got to go."

David followed her outside. "Do you want to go out sometime?" he asked.

Candle frowned, thinking she didn't want him showing up the ranch. "I don't know."

"Look, I work at the Lakes Country Club. I can use the pool after hours. Come by and we'll go swimming," David suggested.

"Okay," Candle said, waving good-bye. In the van, Bane and Ralphie glared at David. Their nostrils opened and closed like they wanted to

17

remember his scent.

Later that night, Candle walked back and forth in her room. Her family had gone running and had asked her to go with them. She said no, wanting to get away from them for a while. But she could not ignore the moon. It called to her.

As she stared at the moon, her muscles rippled and cramped, making her fall on her knees. Silver fur grew from her skin and pointy ears pushed up through her skull as her face grew into a long snout.

When the change was complete, her eyes glowed yellow. She leaped through the open window onto the roof, then onto the ground below.

Her nose twitched as she smelled the desert night air. The moonlight felt good on her back as she ran through the darkness. She heard every sound that the small birds and animals made.

Chapter 4

The next morning when David arrived at the golf course, Tomas was sitting in a golf cart waiting for him. " What's up?" David asked, shutting the door on his pickup.

"We're on cleanup detail," Tomas answered. "We're also supposed to keep an eye out for Jones, the night watchman. His wife called. He never went home last night."

"He probably got drunk and is sleeping it off somewhere," David said as he hopped into the cart.

"Remember that time a golfer found Jones sleeping it off in a sand bunker?" Tomas laughed.

They drove through the golf course toward the man-made lake. As they got closer to the water, David couldn't believe his eyes. Dead ducks and geese lay everywhere.

"Biggs wants this cleaned up before he lets the first group of golfers out on the course," Tomas said. He handed David rubber gloves and a garbage bag.

"What did this?" David asked. He knelt by a large dead goose. David's stomach felt sick. He stood up and took several deep breaths.

"Biggs thinks it was coyotes," Tomas said, putting on his gloves.

"The pack would have to be huge. Besides, coyotes only kill to eat, not for the fun of it," David said. He wished his stomach would settle down.

"Maybe it's wolves," Tomas said. He dropped a dead bird into the bag.

"They don't kill for fun, either," David said.

"Well, I don't think a human did this. Do you?" Tomas asked. He pointed to a duck with its body torn.

"No, I don't. This is really weird, man," David answered.

20

"Gives me the creeps," Tomas said. He tied up a full bag and reached for another one.

The boys picked up dead birds for over an hour. When they were done, Tomas hooked up a hose and sprayed the grass.

As David got into the cart, he saw Candle's brother, Bane, and her cousin, Ralphie, walking up the path.

"Seems like we meet again," Bane said. He acted like he enjoyed watching the boys clean up the awful mess. His dark eyes looked sideways at the lake, then at the bags on the cart.

"Can I help you?" David asked.

"Looks like you already did," said Ralphie with a laugh.

Bane gave his cousin a look like he wanted him to shut up.

"What are you talking about?" David asked, suddenly uneasy.

"Forget it. Ralphie talks to hear himself talk. He doesn't make sense most of the time," Bane joked. "Look, I think we got off to a bad start last night."

David relaxed and shook Bane's hand.

"We're just looking around. We might sign up for golf lessons," Bane said.

"We are?" Ralphie asked.

Bane laughed and gave his cousin's shoulder a hard squeeze.

"The pro club is up that path," Tomas said. He pointed in the direction of the clubhouse.

"See you around," David said. He and Tomas climbed into the cart. Bane nodded.

At the garbage area, they unloaded the bags of dead birds into the trash bin. David told Tomas how he'd met Bane and Ralphie the night before. He also told him about Candle. "She is so beautiful. I hope she comes by."

"You could always drive over to the

ranch and see her," Tomas suggested. He jumped into the cart and waited as David climbed in, too.

"I don't think she wants me showing up at her place." David said.

"I guess we should go wash up and see what Biggs wants us to do next," said Tomas. He dropped his gloves into the trash bin.

David agreed, glancing at the desert. Nothing seemed to move except the heat waves shimmering in the air.

As he turned back toward Tomas, a patch of blue caught his eye. He pointed to the edge of the driving range. "Is that a body down there?"

Tomas drove the cart down the road that ran next to the driving range. The cart ran over old golf balls and raised clouds of dust.

"It's Old Man Jones," David said, jumping from the cart. He knelt next to Jones who lay curled up on the grass, clutching a whiskey bottle. The old man was snoring.

"We'd better wake him up," David said, giving the old man a shake. "We don't want him getting hit with range balls."

Jones woke with a start. "Get away from me!" he screamed. His eyes were wide with terror.

"It's just us, Jones," Tomas said, trying to quiet the old man.

"I saw them!" cried Jones. He hugged his empty bottle and stared at the boys.

"Saw what, Jones?" David asked.

"Werewolves," he whispered. "I saw werewolves."

David grinned. "Werewolves, that's a good one," he said to himself. He helped the old man to his feet.

"I saw them," Jones whispered again. "Werewolves with bloody fangs."

Chapter 5

Candle spent the next few days in her room, feeling unhappy. She felt cursed. She could be a teenage girl most of the time, but when the moon was full, she had no choice but to become her other self. Once she'd been proud of who she was, but that was when her father lived and ruled the pack.

Thinking everyone had left for an evening run, Candle went downstairs. Bane was lying on a couch.

"I thought you went out," Candle said, stopping in the living room hall.

Bane looked up. "House arrest. No night running for the cousins and me for the rest of the month."

"Well, what you did at the golf course lake was sickening," Candle said. She was glad that Sonny Wendig was punishing the boys. Bane and Ralphie

25

had put the whole family in danger with their crazy actions.

"Like you weren't in the shadows drooling," Bane snarled. "You're just upset because your new friend David had to clean up the mess."

"Shut up," Candle said, walking toward the kitchen.

"At least I'm not ashamed of who I am!" Bane yelled. He ran after her.

Candle opened then closed the refrigerator. "Why doesn't Mom buy some food?" She opened a cupboard and took out a jar of peanut butter.

Bane sat on a kitchen chair. "Mom's too busy being nice to Sonny. She wants to be the lead girl in the pack again. But you're the one Sonny really wants."

Candle spread peanut butter on bread. "He can forget it. I'm not going to fight Mom or *any* female for him."

Bane grinned. "You can't refuse to fight, you know. And this weekend,

26

there *will* be a fight in the barn."

"If I don't change into my wolf self, they can't make me fight," Candle said quietly to herself.

She glanced out the window. The old thermometer nailed to the window frame read 113 degrees. The sun was setting, dropping the temperature a couple of degrees, but not enough to be comfortable.

"Make me a sandwich," Bane said, pouring the last of the lemonade into a glass.

"Make it yourself," Candle said. She took his lemonade and headed for her room.

When it was dark, Candle ran the 2 miles from the house to the golf course. When she got there, she walked right in. A boy she didn't know sat by the pool.

"Hi," said David. He pulled himself out of the pool, grinning widely.

"Hi. I hope it's okay that I'm here,"

she said, looking at David's friend.

"Sure, this is my friend Tomas Alvarez. We work together," David said.

Tomas gave David a look of approval. "Well, I was just going," he said. "Nice to meet you, Candle."

"Don't go because of me," Candle said.

"Yeah, just go," David laughed.

Tomas grinned and grabbed his clothes. "Actually, I was only hanging around in case David needed saving."

David laughed again.

The click of the gate as Tomas left sounded loud in the silence. Candle and David looked at each other, then away, both feeling suddenly shy.

"Let's swim," David said. He dove into the pool.

Candle slipped off her clothes. She was wearing a white bikini that showed off her slim figure. She walked to the edge of the pool and did a perfect dive.

28

Candle and David swam and later sat talking in the hot tub. Candle gave David a carefully worded story about her human life. She knew he'd never understand if she told him about her *other* life.

David told her about his job. He talked about his pickup truck and how he was saving money to get new tires and a paint job.

They got back into the pool and swam and splashed around. Candle liked David. He was easy to talk to and he was cute. He made her laugh. For a while, she forgot her family.

Candle hung onto the side of the pool. David leaned toward her. Before he could kiss her, a wolf howled. Candle became tense. The wolf howled again, joined by another seconds later.

Candle climbed out of the pool. " There are a lot of coyotes out here," she lied.

"Or wolves. My dad says there are

signs of wolves moving into the desert," David explained. "And Old Man Jones, the night watchman, says he saw werewolves."

"Werewolves? That's pretty hard to believe," Candle said, acting surprised. Inside, she realized that the local people knew about them. She put on her clothes.

David laughed. "Jones is a drunk. He sees all sorts of things." He slipped on his clothes, too.

The wolves yipped like a chorus of barking dogs. Candle recognized Bane and Ralphie's voices and realized they followed her scent. "I've got to go."

"Did you drive?" David asked, as they started for the gate.

"Mom dropped me off," she lied.

"I'll give you a ride," David said.

The wolves howled again. They sounded close. Candle grabbed David's hand. She didn't want anything to happen to him.

Chapter 6

David watched Candle walk away into the darkness. She had made him stop and let her out before they got to her house. He wondered why she didn't want him to drive her all the way, but he didn't argue.

He put his truck in gear and headed back toward the highway. Warm air blew in through the open windows. He could smell the desert plants and the day's leftover heat mixed with dust.

He was a mile from the highway when he realized something was wrong with his front tire. He stopped and climbed out to look at it. It was almost flat.

"This is just great. I'm miles from town," David grumbled. He kicked the tire.

He knew he'd have to walk to the

highway and try to get someone to give him a ride.

Suddenly, David heard a howl. He told himself that wild animals were scared of humans, but he grabbed a crowbar from under the seat. He thought he might as well be safe, and he slammed the door.

As David walked, he kept looking into the blackness of the desert. A couple of times, he thought he heard something moving through the dry brush. His heart raced. He told himself it was probably rabbits, but he imagined wolves with bloody fangs.

Then something moved onto the road. David stopped. Two wolves, as big as men, blocked the road. David gripped the crowbar tighter. The smaller wolf carried a dead dog in its mouth. David felt sick and scared at the same time.

The larger wolf, silver and black, stared at David, unafraid. It growled

The larger silver and black wolf glared at David, unafraid.

33

and took a step toward him.

"Get out of here!" David screamed. He waved the crowbar, hoping to scare the animals. The large wolf stayed right where it was, baring its fangs.

Let's go, then, David thought. He got up his courage to fight. "One of us is going to lose, and it's not going to be me," he whispered.

As the wolf jumped at him, David swung the crowbar, hitting the beast on the left side of its face. The wolf yelped with pain as blood poured from the wound.

David raised the crowbar to swing again, but the injured wolf stepped back. It looked at David for a minute before turning and running off into the desert. The smaller wolf followed, carrying the dead dog.

David's heart pounded wildly as he ran in the direction of the highway. He wasn't about to wait for the wolves to return.

Chapter 7

The next morning, David told Tomas about the wolves. "After I hit him with the crowbar, they both took off," David said.

"Good thing you had that crowbar," Tomas said.

"Dad says I'm lucky. It's probably the only thing that saved my life," David said. He went from cart to cart, putting scorecards and pencils in their holders as they spoke.

Tomas stood next to a large garbage can, filling plastic containers with a mixture of sand and grass seed. The golfers used it to fix the lawn if their club dug up grass when they swung. " What else did your dad say about the wolves?"

"Well, he's surprised. There haven't been wolves in this area for hundreds

35

of years. And the ones who used to live in this desert were small, like German shepherds. The one that attacked me must have weighed at least 150 pounds," David said.

"That's man-size," Tomas said. He put the lid back on the garbage can and picked up several plastic containers of grass and sand.

David also picked up some containers, and they began placing them in the carts. "Dad thinks the wolf is someone's pet. It sure wasn't scared of me."

"Or maybe," Tomas said, "those wolves that attacked you weren't really wolves."

David looked at Tomas for a second and then grinned. "Don't tell me you believed Old Man Jones's story about werewolves!"

Tomas frowned, "It's a possibility."

"Yeah, in books and movies. It's more likely those wolves are pets that were trained to be attack dogs." David put the last of the containers in the cart's holder. "Look, can you help me get a tire and then drive me out to my pickup after work?"

Just then a pickup truck, followed by a black van, were driven into the parking lot. "Isn't that your pickup?" Tomas asked.

David turned, surprised. "Yeah." As he and Tomas started for the parking lot, Sonny Wendig and Candle climbed out of David's pickup.

"Hey, thanks!" David cried, seeing Candle. She smiled and quickly introduced Sonny Wendig.

"We found your truck and thought you might need it," Sonny Wendig said. He put out his hand to shake.

"Thanks," David said. He glanced from Candle to Sonny. He hoped she hadn't gotten in trouble.

Sonny threw him the keys and headed for the van. "Come on, Candle," he growled.

"I'll call you in a couple of days," Candle whispered.

An unhappy-looking Bane sat behind the wheel of the van. As the vehicle drove out of the lot, David and Tomas saw a large white bandage covering Bane's left cheek.

"Did you see the bandage on her brother's face? It was on the left side, too," Tomas said.

"Yeah, so?" David asked. His mind was on Candle and when he would see her again.

"The wolf!" Tomas said excitedly. " You said you hit the wolf on the left side of the face."

"You think Bane is a werewolf?" David said. He shook his head at his friend's wild imagination. As they went back to work, David couldn't stop thinking that maybe Tomas was right.

Chapter 8

Back at the ranch, Candle ran up the porch stairs. Sonny Wendig and Bane followed her into the house.

"How did it go?" Lucinda asked, coming from the kitchen.

"Fine," Candle said angrily. It annoyed her that her mother always thought something terrible would happen when they were around humans.

"Want some coffee and cake?" Lucinda asked.

Sonny growled. "The kids are out of control, Lucinda. There will be a meeting tonight in the barn."

"A meeting? But no human has been killed!" Lucinda cried. Her dark eyes widened with fear.

"I wouldn't be so sure about that," Sonny said. He stared at Bane.

"We've killed a few dogs and some birds. So what?" Bane said.

"You killed family pets? Is that where you got that gash in your face, Bane?" Lucinda asked sharply.

Bane stared at them stubbornly.

"Tonight, nine o'clock, in the barn," Sonny said as he left.

Candle walked over to Bane, sticking her face close to his. Claws grew from her fingers, ready to scratch. "What happened last night with David?"

Bane shrugged. "I don't know. You're the one who was with him."

Lucinda growled. "You were with a human boy? What did you tell him?"

"Nothing, Mother. I'm not stupid!" Candle yelled. "We're supposed to make friends, right?" She knew it was impossible. She felt caught between two worlds—wolf and human.

"You need a mate of your own kind, Candle," Lucinda said. "Some

40

Turning into a wolf was sweet relief for Candle.

members of the pack say you should now be the lead female. Maybe you and Sonny should be the 'top dogs'."

Bane laughed and Lucinda turned on him, swatting him with her hand. "And you need to learn your place."

Candle was horrified. She wanted to be normal, not joined for life with another werewolf. Anger raced through her veins like fire. She ran from the house and into the desert. Tears ran down her face.

Out beyond the ranch, where no one could see her, Candle bent over. Her spine began to stretch as her tail grew. Turning into a wolf was sweet relief. She ran on all fours, the hot desert air ruffling her fur.

A lizard ran to safety beneath a rock as Candle trotted toward the mountains. Tiny birds chirped under the dry bushes. They all ran as she got closer. Candle laughed, thinking how easy it would be to catch one of the birds to eat. She felt strong with animal power.

When she reached the mountains, she sniffed the air. Smelling no humans, she pushed her way past old timbers and went into an old, empty cave.

Panting from the heat, she lay on her belly on the cold dirt. With her head on her paws, she tried to sort out her thoughts.

She liked David. She felt like a normal teenager around him, but could she really give up being a werewolf? She didn't know.

She barked, listening to her voice echo in the cave. Suddenly tired, she curled up and went to sleep.

It was night when Candle left the cave and started trotting toward the ranch. She was starving. She heard a noise in a nearby bush. It was a ground squirrel. Without thinking, she jumped on it and quickly ate it.

Again, Candle heard something. This time the animal was bigger and it was running. She stopped. Her nose twitched. Then she saw a black wolf. She wondered what Ralphie was doing out here. She stepped into his path.

"Candle?" Ralphie said with surprise.

"Where are you going in such a hurry?" Candle asked. She bared her teeth, threatening him.

Ralphie hung his tail between his legs to show that he didn't want to fight. "I'm leaving the pack."

"Why?" she asked, not at all surprised. She knew if Ralphie had done something to put the pack in danger, he wouldn't take his punishment.

"I can't go to the meeting tonight," Ralphie said. "So I'm moving on." He couldn't look into her eyes.

"What did you do?" Candle asked. She knew it was something really bad.

"I wasn't the only one," Ralphie said in a fearful voice.

Candle snarled and stepped toward her cousin. She was losing her patience.

Ralphie stepped backwards, fear showing in his eyes. "We just got carried away. First it was birds, then the neighbors' dogs. Last night after your human friend chased us off, we killed an old man at the golf course."

Candle was horrified. Killing humans was a crime that was punished by the killer being forced out of the pack, or even by death. "What about my friend?"

"Bane wants to kill him," Ralphie said nervously.

"Why? Because David likes me?"

"Yeah. Bane doesn't want anyone leaving the pack," Ralphie said.

Candle howled like she'd been hurt. She suddenly thought of her brother as a power-hungry animal. She growled, " Leave, Ralphie, before I hurt you!"

Ralphie whined, then started running toward the mountains.

Chapter 9

It was dark when David got back from getting gas for the lawn mowers. The pro shop and surrounding area were lit up like a movie set.

"What's going on?" David asked, walking over to Tomas, who stood in the garage area.

"A couple of golfers found the body of Old Man Jones lying in the bushes near the sixth green. The police have come and gone already," Tomas explained, looking scared.

"How did he die?" David asked, thinking alcohol had killed him.

"The police haven't got a clue. Jones was ripped apart pretty badly. You almost couldn't tell who it was," Tomas said with a shiver. "We should tell the police about Jones seeing werewolves."

David frowned and shook his head.

"Oh, right. Like anyone would believe us."

"We've got to do something," Tomas said."

"Let's go," David said, heading back toward his truck.

"Aren't you going to put the gas cans back in the garage?" Tomas asked.

"No time," David said. The expression on his face was serious. He started to drive the truck as Tomas was still getting in.

David drove to the main highway. Instead of turning left for town, he turned right toward the ranch.

"This is not a good idea. That Bane guy could be the werewolf," Tomas said. His eyes were wide with fear.

"I've been thinking the same thing," David answered. "That's why I've got to warn Candle about her brother."

"Maybe she's one, too. Did you ever think of that?" Tomas said.

David shook his head. "Candle is

not a werewolf."

"How do you know?" Tomas asked. He rolled up his window as David turned the pickup down the road that led to the ranch.

"I just know," David said. He added angrily, "She's too sweet and gentle, okay?"

"Okay," Tomas answered. "We should have silver bullets if we're going werewolf hunting."

"Silver bullets?" David looked at Tomas.

"I read somewhere that only silver bullets can kill a werewolf," Tomas explained.

"Well, we don't have any silver bullets." David said angrily.

He knew he was taking his anger out on his friend, but he couldn't help it. He couldn't let his fear take over or he'd turn the truck around and drive it back to town.

Lights showed in the ranch house

windows and in the windows of the outer buildings. David parked in front of the main house.

"What are you going to say?" Tomas asked.

"I'm going to give them back the tire they put on my truck and thank them. Then I'm going to ask Candle if I can talk to her," David said. He gave Tomas a serious look.

Tomas nodded nervously.

David got out of his truck. He leaned the tire next to the porch and knocked on the front door. An older woman opened the door. David guessed it was Candle's mother.

"Hi, Mrs. Selky?" David asked. He gave her his best smile.

"Yes?"

"I'm Candle's friend, David Payne. I was wondering if I could talk to her."

Lucinda frowned and looked over her shoulder, like she was looking for help.

"No, you can't," said Bane. He stepped in front of his mother like a bodyguard.

"Bane just means she's not here right now," said Sonny Wendig from the bottom of the porch stairs.

David looked from Bane to Sonny. "I brought back the tire you put on my truck, sir," David said.

"You didn't have to return it," Sonny said. "It's an old one we found in the barn. Just being neighborly." He smiled warmly, but he seemed cautious, too.

David glanced over his shoulder at Bane who glared at him. He went down the stairs to where Sonny stood and held out his hand to shake. "Well, thanks. I appreciate your help."

David almost cried out at the strength of Sonny's grip. "Please tell Candle I came by. Maybe she could call me when she gets back," David said, looking back at Lucinda.

"Not tonight. We're having a family meeting," Lucinda said. She then added, "Tomorrow. I'll have her call you tomorrow." Bane shoved his mother back into the house while Sonny Wendig's grin disappeared.

"We're having one of our little family parties tonight. We eat and sing old songs. Candle will have to invite you to one sometime," Sonny said. He acted like it was no big deal.

"Well, thanks again for bringing my truck to the golf course," David said, getting into his truck. He gripped the wheel to keep his hands from shaking as he backed out and turned around. His heart was beating like a drum.

"Weirdos," Tomas whispered. Looking out the side mirror as they drove away, he was relieved no one followed them.

David took a deep breath. "I've got a feeling they were all lying. I think Candle is in the house."

"I saw someone in the upstairs window," Tomas said. "Maybe they're holding her prisoner."

David glanced sideways at Tomas, thinking he might be right. He turned the truck off the highway. He switched off the truck lights when they reached the dry brush.

"What are you doing?" Tomas asked.

"We're going to wait a couple of hours. Then we're going to go back," David said. All he thought of was Candle and how he would save her.

Chapter 10

The moon was high when David and Tomas walked toward the Double R Ranch. "Why are we taking these cans of gas?" Tomas asked.

"If there are wolves at the ranch, we can burn them out," David said, keeping his voice low.

"Oh, so now you *do* believe in werewolves," Tomas said.

"I don't know what I believe. I just want to see Candle and make sure she's all right," David answered.

"I wish we had some weapons. We're defenseless, man," Tomas said. His voice shook with fear.

"If you want to go back, then go," David said. He was having trouble trying to stay brave himself.

As they neared the ranch house, a wolf howled, long and loud. Then,

53

another wolf began to howl, and another until the night was filled with the cries of a wolf pack. The ranch was dark except for the light peeking from under the barn door.

Moving quietly, David and Tomas made their way to the side of the old barn. David peeked into a crack and could see inside. What he saw gave him chills. His legs felt weak.

Inside the barn, werewolves formed a circle around two more large werewolves—Sonny and Bane. The fur on their necks stood up, and their teeth were bared as they faced each other. Sonny growled, then Bane growled. They circled around each other, snarling and snapping.

Suddenly, Bane jumped at Sonny, sinking his teeth into Sonny's neck. The other males started fighting, too. The growling and snarling grew louder as all the werewolves fought each other.

David searched the barn for Candle.

54

Suddenly, he saw her. She was standing behind a bale of hay, watching. She was the only human in the barn. Tears streaked her pretty face. When an older black werewolf jumped at a younger silver-colored wolf, Candle screamed and ran out of the barn.

Without thinking, David grabbed Candle's arm as she ran past. He pulled her down into the grass next to him.

"David? What are you doing here?" Candle gasped.

"I was worried about you," David whispered.

Candle choked back a sob. "You have to get out of here. They'll kill you if they find you."

Tomas picked up his can of gasoline and began throwing gas on the barn. David grabbed his can and went in the other direction. "Candle, lock the barn door," David whispered.

Candle looked at the fighting through the crack in the wall. Sonny had Bane by the throat. Her mother, Lucinda, was fighting with one of Candle's female cousins. She felt only disgust for her family and herself. She went silently to the front of the barn and pushed the wooden lock in place, locking the wolves inside.

Inside the barn, the werewolves continued to snarl and growl as they fought among themselves.

Somewhere Tomas had found an old newspaper. He rolled it and lit it. Then he ran around the barn lighting the walls. The dry wood burst into flame.

Candle screamed and started for the barn. David grabbed her and held her tightly as the barn exploded in flames. Smoke poured from the cracks in the walls as flames shot through the roof.

"We've got to get out of here!" Tomas cried, running to where David stood holding Candle. They heard howls of pain and fear coming from inside the blazing barn.

Suddenly, burning werewolves broke through the flaming door and ran into the desert night. Seconds later, the barn's roof fell in.

The gaping hole in the barn door showed the blazing fire inside the barn. More werewolves escaped, howling into the desert darkness.

Candle broke away from David and began running toward the burning building. "Mother!" Candle screamed, seeing Lucinda and Bane trapped under a burning beam. Sonny lay nearby, not moving.

"Candle, wait!" David yelled, running after her. As he caught up with her, she turned and growled at him. David stepped back, horrified, as Candle continued to change into a wolf.

Her spine bent and twisted until she fell to the ground on all fours. She swung her silver-colored head in David' s direction. She saw the horror on his face. She now knew where she belonged. With a flying jump, Candle threw herself into the burning barn.

"Candle!" David screamed. He wanted to stop what was happening and yet knew he couldn't. His eyes filled with tears as he stared at the raging fire.

"You okay?" asked Tomas, coming to stand by him.

David nodded, wondering if anything would ever be okay again.

The distant howl of a lone wolf broke the silence. Another wolf howled in answer. David and Tomas looked at each other. Somewhere, out in the desert, a werewolf was searching for the rest of its pack.